AF610634

Published by Canon Press
P.O. Box 8729, Moscow, Idaho 83843
800.488.2034 | www.canonpress.com

Cited page numbers come from the Canon Classics edition (2016), www.canonpress.com/books/canon-classics.

Cover design by James Engerbretson
Cover illustration by Forrest Dickison
Interior design by Valerie Anne Bost and James Engerbretson

Printed in the United States of America.

Library of Congress Cataloging-in-Publication Data
Ryan, Amanda, author.
The secret garden worldview guide / Amanda Ryan.
Moscow, Idaho : Canon Press, [2018]
LCCN 2019011348 | ISBN 9781947644212 (paperback : alk. paper)
LCSH: Burnett, Frances Hodgson, 1849-1924. Secret garden.
Classification: LCC PS1214.S43 R93 2018 | DDC 813/.4--dc23
LC record available at https://lccn.loc.gov/2019011348

A free end-of-book test and answer key are available for download at www.canonpress.com/ClassicsQuizzes

18 19 20 21 22 23 9 8 7 6 5 4 3

WORLDVIEW GUIDE

THE SECRET GARDEN

Amanda Ryan

CONTENTS

Introduction 1

The World Around 3

About the Author 5

What Other Notables Said 9

Setting, Characters, and Plot Summary 11

Worldview Analysis 15

Quotables 25

21 Significant Questions and Answers 27

Further Discussion and Review 35

Taking the Classics Quiz 39

INTRODUCTION

The Secret Garden is Frances Hodgson Burnett's most famous novel. It came at a time when the romantic child-character of previous children's literature began to disappear and gave way to more "realistic depictions." The Secret Garden is often praised for pioneering, the character of the flawed-child. It tells the story of two spoiled, selfish children who are healed and transformed through the magic of Spring.

THE WORLD AROUND

The Secret Garden was published as a serial in *The American Magazine* in 1910, and later in its entirety in 1911. At this time, the British Empire was at its zenith. Its colonies included parts of Africa and China, India, Canada, and Australia, to name a few. Across the ocean, America, which had recovered from the after-effects of its civil war, was booming. Theodore Roosevelt just finished two terms chock-full of progressive policies which expanded the navy and thus increased the country's international influence. The country was experiencing a great influx of immigrants and technology. Transportation advances zoomed. Henry Ford mass-produced his Model T, making automobiles affordable to the middle class while Orville and Wilbur Wright built and piloted their machine-powered aircraft, conquering the skies. The inventions of Thomas Edison, Alexander Graham Bell, and others were being widely implemented across the country. America was teeming with new people, new tools, and new ideas..

During this prosperous time, America also saw the rise of new and zany religions. Mary Baker Eddy, a woman with the face of Abe Lincoln, founded the Christian Science movement in an attempt to rectify aspects of Calvinism she found distasteful. Theosophy, Anthroposophy, and other New Age movements were popular as well, influencing authors like Frank L. Baum and H.P. Lovecraft.

At this point, children's literature was already an established genre, having evolved from the fairy tales of the Brothers Grimm (1785-1863) and Hans Christian Anderson (1805-1875) to the didactic morality tales of such writers as Revd. W. Caros Wilson and Martha Finley (author of the *Elsie Dinsmore* series). The "Golden Age of Children's Literature" began in the 1850s, as authors explored notions of childhood and children in their characters. When *The Secret Garden* debuted, the figure of the plucky, winsome orphan girl was en vogue, as can be seen in the classics *Rebecca of Sunnybrook* by Kate Douglas Wiggins (1903), Burnett's own *A Little Princess* (1905), and *Anne of Green Gables* by Lucy Maud Montgomery (1908). The Secret Garden would introduce another orphan character, but one that is very different from her predecessors.

ABOUT THE AUTHOR

Francis Hodgson Burnett was born on November 24th, 1849, in Manchester, England, to Edwin and Eliza Hodgson. When Frances' father died of epilepsy, her mother packed up her five children and immigrated to America to live with her brother.

In the Civil War-wracked state of Tennessee, the Hodgsons struggled to maintain their livelihood and Frances consistently did what she could to help the family financially. When she was eighteen-years-old she wrote and submitted a short love story to a magazine called *Godey's Lady's Book.* The story was accepted for publication and Frances was paid a whopping thirty-five dollars. Thus began what would escalate into a successful and lucrative literary career.

In 1873 Francis married Swan Burnett, a childhood friend and aspiring ophthalmologist whose unfortunate first name Frances would fondly avoid with alternate nicknames in her letters and writing. Frances maintained her writing throughout their marriage and continued the trend of providing financially, putting her husband through medical school via the payments on her novels. She had two sons with Swan, Vivian and Lionel, whom she doted on in a way likely similar to her depiction of Cedric Errol in *Little Lord Fauntleroy.*

Burnett first won acclaim as a novelist for *That Lass O' Lowrie*, published in 1877. In 1883, she wrote the novel *Through One Administration*, the story of an unhappy marriage which was celebrated for its realism.

Although she had a splendid literary career, her personal life was not as shiny. As Frances became a literary celebrity, she was often at events and parties, away from her home and children. She loved the social aspects of her literary fame, though they put a severe strain on her marriage. Burnett was often plagued by anxiety and depression, which prompted her to seek mind-healing help from the creepy folks at Christian Science centers. In 1890 her fifteen-year-old son Lionel tragically died of consumption. After her son's death, Frances mainly focused on writing children's stories, much to the chagrin of the literati and all the fans of her promising, more serious work in adult fiction. She divorced Swan Burnett, and scandalously jumped into marriage with a man ten years younger than herself, only to divorce him two years later.

During the last decade of her life, she penned her two most famous novels: *A Little Princess* in 1905, and *The*

Secret Garden in 1911. Although she continued to dabble in adult fiction later in life, it was her children's fiction that gave her the enduring recognition of a gifted storyteller.

WHAT OTHER NOTABLES SAID

When first published, *The Secret Garden* was not instantly recognized as the classic it is today. The book initially met with some disapproval from the critics. One reviewer from *The Athenaeum* said the story was "over-sentimental and dealing almost wholly with abnormal people."[1]

Despite this critical reception, the book persisted in being a favorite among children and continues to inspire many. Katherine Paterson, author of the contemporary children's book Bridge to Terabithia, called The Secret Garden "more of a mystical experience than a book." "I think the reason so many of us have loved that book," She explained, "is precisely because we are homesick for a garden we have never visited."[2]

---

1 *American Library Association Booklist*, vol. 8 (October 1911): 76.

2 Katherine Paterson, *Read for Your Life: Speeches and Writings of Katherine Paterson* (Boston: Clarion Books, 2011), 10.

SETTING, CHARACTERS AND PLOT SUMMARS

- *Setting:* The story begins in India but is soon relocated to Northern England. Mary goes to live with her uncle at Misselthwaite Manor, a mysterious mansion isolated on the moors of the county of Yorkshire, not too far south of Scotland.
- *Mary Lennox:* Our protagonist, a spoiled, sour-faced, ten-year-old girl.
- *Ayah:* Mary's Indian nursemaid.
- *Mr. and Mrs. Lennox:* Mary's unloving, neglectful parents.
- *The Crawfords:* The family Mary briefly stays with in India before her journey to England.
- *Archibald Craven:* Mary's uncle who is heartbroken, depressed, and reclusive after the death of his wife.

- *Colin Craven:* Mary's cousin and a tantrum-throwing hypochondriac. Considered a second protagonist.
- *Mrs. Medlock:* the spinsterly, no-nonsense housekeeper of Misselthwaite.
- *Martha Sowerby:* the relentlessly cheerful servant at Misselthwaite who helps knock sense into Mary.
- *Dickon Sowerby:* Martha's brother and animal tamer. He helps Mary cultivate the secret garden.
- *Susan Sowerby:* mother extraordinaire to Martha, Dickon, and ten others. Her wise motherly presence is felt throughout the story, influencing both Mary and Colin.
- *Robin:* one of Mary's first friends who shows her the key to the secret garden.
- *Ben Weatherstaff:* the gardener at Misselthwaite and the children's confidante when it comes to the garden.
- *Dr. Craven:* Mr. Craven's brother and Colin's doctor.
- *Nurse:* we don't get her name but she assists Dr. Craven and takes care of Colin's medical needs, although somewhat reluctantly and with frequent smirks at his behavior.

The Secret Garden is the story of two spoiled, miserable children whose lives are magically matured into happiness and health. Mary Lennox, a sour ten-year-old living in British-ruled Colonial India, becomes an orphan through a typhoid epidemic and is sent to England to live with her Uncle and cousin at Misselthwaite Manor, a mysterious castle surrounded by moors. There, Mary discovers that Misselthwaite has been darkened by the death of her aunt, Mrs. Craven. Tragically, Mrs. Craven's death was precipitated by her falling off a swing in her favorite garden. Mary's uncle, never able to overcome his grief, lives in self-appointed exile, rarely visiting Misselthwaite or his son, and commanding that the garden his wife had loved so much be locked up and untouched.

Despite this gloomy setting, Mary encounters a cheery crew of servants at Misselthwaite, whose sensible English treatment (along with their heavy Yorkshire accents) helps to shake her out of her brattiness. As she discovers the truth about herself (that she is not much fun), she begins to make friends and becomes interested in the world around her. When a friendly robin leads her to the abandoned key that opens the door to the locked garden, she quickly gets to work tending it. With the aide of her moor-wandering friend, Dickon, flower buds begin to sprout.

One night, after hearing eerie cries from somewhere in the castle, she discovers the existence of her cousin Colin, a seeming cripple and invalid who is as equally spoiled and unpleasant as she had once been. Mary befriends Colin and challenges him out of his sickly delusions. She brings

Colin to the secret garden and there Colin's character and health improve. About the time Colin learns how to walk, Susan Sowerby, the uber-influential mother of Dickon and Martha, writes to Archibald Craven urging him to come home. Archibald returns to Misselthwaite and is joyously reunited with his son.

WORLDVIEW ANALYSIS

"The most misused word in the language is 'realism,'" Frances Burnett once remarked. "It has come to stand solely for all that is hideous, sordid and repulsive in life. One would think, to judge from the way in which the word is bandied about, that no real things were beautiful or good."[3] In reaction to the idealism and sentimentality that marked Victorian literature, what became fashionable was the portrayal of discontents, anxieties, and injustices— sins that make people easily recognizable to each other. According to this trend, what was most realistic and meaningful in the world was its darkness, grit, and depravity and, therefore, was most worthy of serious storytelling.

After decades of a successful writing career, Burnett's work had received both admiration for its realism, as well as criticism for a lack of it. *The Secret Garden*, in particular,

---

3 "Gloomy Plays Evil, Says Mrs. Burnett," *Chicago Examiner*, February 14, 1909, 1.

was often lauded for the "psychological realism" of Mary and Colin, but sniffed at when the flowers began to grow and the magical healing takes place. Critics approved of the winter, but not of the spring.

In an interview given two years before publishing *The Secret Garden*, Burnett preemptively defends her work by seeking to widen our definition of realism. She remarks: "A rose, a spring day, the sun, kindness, tolerance, nobility, unselfishness—these are as real as poverty and sin and hopelessness." These observations help illuminate Burnett's possible motivation for writing her most enduring and beloved work. In *The Secret Garden*, Burnett shows the ugliness of human behavior and then, as if to shake her fists at her critics, overcomes human depravity with the power of Spring. Although her depictions of rebirth deserve criticism, the story's message is one that Christians should heed—beauty and goodness will always triumph over the harsh "realism" of Winter.

Burnett starts with the gritty from the story's get-go as she introduces her reader to one of her protagonists, Mary Lennox, a spoiled little degenerate who needs to change. The conflict of the story arises out of Mary's need for transformation, a simple and common enough tale. But there's a hitch—not only does Mary not know how to change, she has no idea that she needs to. "She did not know she was disagreeable. She often thought that other people were, but she did not know that she was so herself"

(p. 11).[4] Although she clearly needs help, she is blinkered to the fact.

It's important to understand how much the story emphasizes Mary's ugliness. She is rotten, inside and out. On page one, she is described as "the most-disagreeable-looking child ever seen," and a little later we are told that "she was not an affectionate child and had never cared much for any one" (pp. 1, 4). She is demanding, easily angered, self-absorbed, and brutal. Despite potential hang-ups over the mythic, innate lovability of orphans, readers are assured, over and over, that there is nothing likeable about Mary.

We might protest that it's not Mary's fault she is the way she is. Her parents are to blame. They are unloving, neglectful, and downright abusive. Although Burnett undoubtedly wants her readers to make this connection, Mary is not ennobled for it. She is not put in a sympathetic light because of the injustices done to her. The reader is not meant to overlook her character deficiencies because her circumstances are pitiable. Wherever the ultimate blame ought to fall, Mary herself is ugly deep down and is left alone to bear the consequences of her character. Furthermore, Mary's transformation did not take place on account of anything good in her. Her character is empty of goodness so that, as we will see, her transformation must come from nothing.

---

4 Page numbers throughout come from the Canon Classics edition of *The Secret Garden* (Moscow, ID: Canon Press, 2016).

After the problem of Mary's character is established, the story proceeds into rebirth and renewal, moving in parallel with the seasons. When Mary's parents die, she moves to a new home, to a new country in the Winter. Though we see no transformation in Mary when she first arrives at Misselthwaite, there she is given a new identity with her Uncle and cousin. Later, we see her character grow as Spring slowly materializes.

The first glimmer of change that appears in Mary is self-knowledge, which has particular ramifications for Mary to see the world as it is. In her initial state of self-absorption, she is unable to see herself truthfully and therefore unable to see those around her and the rest of creation truthfully. When the crusty gardener, Ben Weatherstaff, tells her she resembles himself—crotchety, bad tempered, and unattractive—Mary is forced to see herself as other do. The narrator explains,

> This was plain speaking, and Mary Lennox had never heard the truth about herself in her life. Native servants always salaamed and submitted to [her] whatever [she] did. She had never thought much about her looks, but she wondered if she looked as unattractive as Ben Weatherstaff.... She actually began to wonder also if she was 'nasty tempered.' She felt uncomfortable. (p. 33)

She had spent most of her life disliking others and, as it turns out, she herself is unlikable and is perhaps at the root of her contentions with others. When the relentlessly cheerful Martha asks her if she likes herself, Mary responds honestly, "Not at all—really. But I never thought of that before" (p. 52). These casual remarks help clear the weeds from Mary's soul. After this realization, she begins to take interest in others, first in the robin and then in Dicken, the garden, and others. The more interest Mary takes in people in front of her, in the food served to her, and the gardens around her, the more conscious she becomes of the world around her. Once she sees herself accurately, she begins to take in her surroundings as they truly are.

Burnett writes about Mary's (and later Colin's) transformation as something as real and frequent as the changing of the seasons. Winter gives way to Spring. Colors appear from the ground and they appear in Mary's once-pale cheeks. Traces of beauty can be seen in the landscape as well as in her character. How exactly did it happen? "One day things weren't there and another they were," says Colin, describing the phenomenon. He goes on to explain,

> "Magic is always pushing and drawing and making things out of nothing, Everything is made out of Magic, leaves and trees, flowers and birds, badgers and foxes and squirrels and people." (p. 194)

The fact that a seed in the grounds combined with sun and water can bring about the glories of Spring can only be explained by one thing—Magic.

The Secret Garden works within a realism where new things come out of nothing, and those are the most real of all. Isn't this the way God works? He takes hold of us, even while we refuse to acknowledge Him, blind to our own need for help, and transforms us, heals us, and bestows loveliness. We contribute nothing. And yet, it cannot be stressed enough, rebirth is only possible through God, which brings us to one of the main problems of the book: who is the Magician behind all the transformations?

Burnett was raised in an Anglican church and attended Christian churches most of her life. However, she was more a secularist and Universalist in word and deed. *The Secret Garden* has many Christian elements and themes, there is also some kookiness to be aware of.

When it comes to the descriptions of the "magic" that changed Mary and healed Colin and brought life to the garden, there is ambiguity as to whom gets the credit. Many argue that the "magic" in *The Secret Garden* is a tip of the hat to the Christian Science movement, which taught that sickness and disease were mere hang-ups of the mind and that one could be healed by pulling oneself up by the bootstraps of positive thoughts. Although Burnett denied association with Christian Science, there remains an undeniable influence and attraction to its ideology in her story.

Colin's narrative gives the clearest example of Christian Science ideas in the story. As his hypochondriac tendencies fall away, he attempts to identify the source of his healing: "Every morning and every evening and as often in the daytime as I can remember I am going to say, 'Magic is in me! Magic is making me well! I am going to be as strong as Dickon'" (p. 194). This little formula—speaking positive affirmations until belief kicks in and unlocks some mental magic that immediately heals a physical malady—is, not to be too dismissive, face-palmingly stupid. There is a health benefit in having a cheerful spirit. Proverbs 17:22 says "a cheerful heart is good medicine but a crushed spirit dries up the bones." But Proverbs does not say that all sickness and disease is a mere trick of the mind and if you but believe good things for yourself long enough you can make them come true. Any child who's ever wish-thought themselves a lifetime supply of ice cream knows Positive Thought is bunk.

When thinking about this dose of the ridiculous in *The Secret Garden*, Christians should keep a couple things in mind. However deeply and seriously Burnett meant Positive Thought to bear on the story, the text itself gives us some permission to dismiss it. Most of these Positive Thought ideas originate from the character Colin, who was so trapped in his own delusions about sickness and dying that no one thought helping him learn how to walk might come in handy. Considering who's saying it, the theory is not presented in a very convincing light. In addition, remember that there was nothing physically wrong with Colin. He was healed of his own cowardice and bad attitude, not of any physical disease.

Besides the presence of Positive Thought, what is most concerning about this story is that Burnett is non-committal when it comes to identifying the source of all goodness brought about at the end of the story. There is definitely a moment of gratitude at the end of the story. When Colin remarks, "I feel as if I want to shout out something—something thankful, joyful!" (p. 221), Ben Weatherstaff suggests they sing the doxology. Mary and Colin have probably never been to church and were never taught whom to thank for the good gifts around them. Dickon teaches the other children the song which thanks "Father, Son, and Holy Spirit", remarking that his "Mother says she believes th'sky larks sings it when they gets up i'th'mornin" (p. 221).

When Susan Sowerby shows up in the garden and is asked if she believed in Magic, she says that she does. But listen to what she says next and you'll hear Burnett's Universalist beliefs reveal themselves through Mama Sowerby's loosey-goosey speech:

> "That I do, lad," she answered. "I never knowed it by that name **but what does th'name matter?** I warrant they call it a different name i'France an' a different one i'Germany. The same thing as set th'seeds swellin' an' th' sun shinin' made thee a well lad an' it's a Good Thing. It isn't like us poor fools as think it matters if us is called out of our names. Th' Big Good Thing doesn't stop to worrit, bless thee. It goes on makin' worlds by th' million—worlds like us. Never thee stop believin' in th' Big Good Thing an' knowin' th' world's full of it—an' call it what tha' likes. Tha' wert singin' to it when I come into th' garden." (pp. 226-27)

There are many troubling things in this paragraph, but let's look at just a few. Susan Sowerby believes that the God of the Bible is the Magician, but says that His name is a moot point. While she is right to recognize that the hand which heals a human heart is the same hand that makes the flowers grow, she is woefully wrong to think that what we call Him is a matter of mere semantics. His name is of infinite importance. Because of course there is no other name under Heaven given to mankind by which we must be saved (Acts 4:12), healed, or transformed except through Jesus Christ.

At the heart of Burnett's story are questions which challenge our ideas of realism and reality. Who makes the flowers grow and causes the seasons to change? Who banishes loneliness and transforms depravity? Are these changes observable in the world and who is responsible for causing them?

Burnett's answer was milquetoast when it came to naming the Giver of all these good things. However, she accurately put her finger on a problem that continues to plague the storytelling world of self-important artistes everywhere—that the darkness defines reality. This kind of understanding of realism denies the power of the Gospel and flies in the face of the way God created the world.

Burnett's instinct in her story is to show us that beauty, goodness, and light are more real than ugliness, evil, and darkness. Although her depictions of goodness are a bit flimsy and sentimental, her instinct is one Christians can benefit from. For Christians, goodness and light should be the governing realities of our lives and stories. While Christians acknowledge the presence of darkness, sin, sickness, and heartache, these are not more "real" than God's beauty, goodness, grace, and truth, all of which are present in this world. In fact, all of creation and Christians themselves testify to the fact that what is most powerful and glorious is the redemption and transformation God has bought for His people and all of creation through His Son. This is a reality that persists through eternity. Death will one day be conquered, sin gone, sickness reversed, loneliness expelled. In contrast, God's loveliness, His goodness displayed in His creation and His people, will live on. Darkness, in God's world, exists to amplify the light, and we can thank God for it.

QUOTABLES

1. “People never like me and I never like people”
~The Secret Garden, p. 30.

2. “Where you tend a rose, my lad, a thistle cannot grow.”
~The Secret Garden, p. 229.

3. “Two worst things as can happen to a child is never to have his own way—or always to have it.”
~The Secret Garden, p. 148.

4. “Might I,” quavered Mary, “might I have a bit of earth?”
~The Secret Garden, p. 97.

5. “Sometimes since I’ve been in the garden I’ve looked up through the trees at the sky and I have had a strange feeling of being happy as if something was pushing and drawing in my chest and making me breathe fast. Magic is always pushing and drawing and making things out of nothing. Everything is made out

of magic, leaves and trees, flowers and birds, badgers and foxes and squirrels and people. So it must be all around us. In this garden— in all the places."

~The Secret Garden, p. 194.

6. "One of the new things people began to find out in the last century was that thoughts—just mere thoughts—are as powerful as electric batteries—as good for one as sunlight is, or as bad for one as poison. To let a sad thought or a bad one get into your mind is as dangerous as letting a scarlet fever germ get into your body. If you let it stay there after it has got in you may never get over it as long as you live... surprising things can happen to anyone who, when a disagreeable or discouraged thought comes into his mind, just has the sense to remember in time and push it out by putting in an agreeable determinedly courageous one. Two things cannot be in one place."

~The Secret Garden, pp. 228-229.

21 SIGNIFICANT QUESTIONS AND ANSWERS

1. How and where is the theme of motherhood seen?

   In some ways, motherhood, and the influence of mothers, is what *The Secret Garden* is all about. Both Mary and Colin have mothers whose absence results in the children's character deficiencies. Someone might point out that both father and mother are responsible for their children. True enough. In this story, however, Mary and Colin are most affected by the loss of their mothers. Mary is most captivated by her mother, whose love of parties and fashion was greater than her love of her child. In Colin's situation, the death of his mother initiates his father's abandonment and the stifling treatment he receives from the people around him.

   In contrast to these failures of motherhood, Susan Sowerby is the mother par excellence whose wisdom and nurturing, even at a distance, strengthen the children throughout much of the story.

2. How does Burnett contrast India to England?

India is hot and desert-like. Nothing grows there. The environment contributes to Mary's sickly constitution and contrary behavior. Not only does the climate make her "hot and languid and weak" (p. 57), but the servants left to look after her operate in a caste system, where Mary is above them and may boss them around, despite her being a child and they adults. Thus, she gets her way all the time and is spoiled. In England, there is fresh air and the servants do not treat her like royalty, which is most healthy for her.

3. Is the way Mary talks about the Indian people racist? Does this make *The Secret Garden* a racist book?

Mary's remarks about the Indian people are obviously demeaning. She says, "You thought I was a native! … They are not people—they're servants who must salaam to you" (pp. 22-23). This talk is problematic for Mary because it reveals genuine racism. However, her talk is not problematic for the story because, given her character at this point in the story, Mary is monstrous in her treatment of all people. Her attitude to other ethnicities is not being held up by the author as virtuous or exemplary and therefore should pose no problems for readers who can discern where to place her speech.

4. Is Martha's talk about "the blacks" racist?

   Although Martha's choice of words might offend a 21st century, hyper-triggered audience, we should approach her behavior with charity, for a couple of reasons. First, though Martha has never interacted with a black person, she has been taught a right view of them. "I've nothin' against th'blacks," says Martha. "When you read about 'em in tracts they're always very religious. You always read as a black's a man an'a brother" (p. 23). Given Martha's cheerful and obviously good character, we should believe what she says. Interestingly, the tracts that Martha references are almost certainly those published by William Wilberforce and his group of abolitionists who tirelessly opposed the slave trade in England's recent history. Those tracts often displayed a black man, in chains, with the words "AM I NOT A MAN AND A BROTHER?," written beneath .

5. What effect does repetition as a literary device achieve in *The Secret Garden*?

   It helps to emphasize a theme or point the author is trying to make. An example is the repetition of how Mary is quite contrary.

6. What is a contrarian and how is Mary like one?

   A contrarian is someone who takes the opposite opinion of the person in front of him or her, no matter what. Mary behaves in this way as a defense mechanism. At the start of the book, we see that

Mary is lonely, yet she refuses to allow others near her. She scorns the company of the Crawford children, as we see when the little boy Basil becomes interested in her gardening game and she tells him to "go away. [she doesn't] want boys" (p. 8). As Mrs. Medlock tells her the story of Mrs. Craven's death, Mary feigns indifference, although she is in fact very interested in the story. "It all sounded so unlike India, and anything new rather attracted her. But she did not intend to look as if she were interested" (p. 12). She reacts to people by taking an opposite stance to protect herself from hurt, but this also keeps her from help.

7. Who is Mary's first friend? Why is this significant?

   Mary's first friend is the Robin, who "remembers" her and "likes" her. Their friendship shows how deeply lonely Mary is and it sets up Mary's close connection to nature.

8. What is significant about the way Mary discovers the key to the secret garden?

   The Robin shows her where the key is buried while looking for a worm and then the wind sweeps the leaves away, revealing the hidden door to the garden. This is clearly a case of magic at work.

9. Describe Dickon's character. What Greek (demi) god is he like?

    Dickon is a super-friend to the flora and the fauna. He talks to birds and other animals and can make anything grow. He also plays wooden pipes. In many ways his character resembles the Greek, goat-footed demi-god, Pan.

10. What are the gothic elements of the book?

    The gloomy, haunted castle, the lonely moors that seem to "cry" when the wind blows, the eerie cries Mary hears in the castle at night, and the invalid kept hidden are all gothic elements of *The Secret Garden.*

11. Do you see any connections between *The Secret Garden* and *Jane Eyre*?

    Both novels share many of the same gothic elements as well as similarities in plot: an orphan girl journeys across the bleak-looking moors to live in a gloomy mansion and discovers, through the strange cries in the night, that someone else is living there.

12. What aspects of the book can be seen as having been influenced from the romantic period?

    One of the most marked romantic features of the book is the idea that children have a special connection with nature. We see this through Mary's friendship with the Robin, Dickon's magical abilities with plants and wildlife, and all the children's relationship with the garden which has a healing and friendship-cultivating influence on them.

13. The garden is often seen as symbolic of Mary's own transformation. Is this symbolism Biblical?

    Mary's slow transformation is highlighted by the changing of the seasons and the landscape around her. When Mary arrives at Misselthwaite, it is winter-grey and gloomy. The moors surrounding her are described as "miles and miles and miles of wild land that nothing grows on but heather and gorse and broom, and nothing lives on but wild ponies and sheep" (p. 17). The new world Mary arrives in is seemingly desolate, gloomy and lonely. Again, we are meant to feel the hopelessness of the situation. As far as anyone can see or tell, there is nothing beautiful about the moor. There is no life to animate it.

14. Why is the name "Craven" fitting for Colin and his father?

    According to Webster's dictionary, to be craven means to be "lacking the least bit of courage: contemptibly fainthearted." Both Colin and his father suffer from cowardice. Archibald cannot face the loss of his wife, and his grief over the potential illnesses of his son, and this cowardly behavior leads to much of the conflicts of Colin's story. Colin would rather hide behind his perceived sickness than exert himself to get better.

15. *The Secret Garden* is often accused of being too didactic and of having elements of the "morality" tale. What evidence is there for this, and does it hinder the story?

    The story is written in the omniscient voice and there are many instances where the narrator gives little asides to comment on a certain character's behavior or explain a certain scene. Burnett's didacticism, however, is subtle, and the story is the main vehicle she uses to teach. This should not be problematic for Christians. As Horace put it, a story's purpose is to instruct and delight, and while a story might fail to do the later, "instructing" is inescapable. Everyone preaches something and no one is so preachy as the one who claim he never preaches and insists on not being preached at.

16. Is Archibald Craven as awful a parent as Mary parents were?

    Yes. While it is understandable for Mr. Craven to grieve the loss of his wife, for him to virtually abandon his son to the care of servants and doctors who spoil him is on par with the neglect that Mary experiences with her parents. The difference between Mr. Craven and Mary's parents is that there is evidence of some affection on Archibald's part for Colin.

17. In chapter twenty-five, Burnett makes use of her omniscient voice and gives us the perspectives of the Robins. Does this "work" with the rest of the story?

On the one hand, it really doesn't work with the rest of the book, since the narrator never bothers to write from the Robin's perspective before, despite many opportunities to do so, and breaks this trend for only one short passage. On the other hand, this passage can be given a pass because it is amusing and charming to see the plot evolving from the Robin's birdseye view.

18. What is Colin's mother's name and what does it reveal?

    Her name is Lilias, which we find out when Archibald is mysteriously called home and he responds, as if to his dead wife. Beyond the obvious, her name reinforces the spiritualist idea that her presence haunts the garden.

19. Is the ending satisfying? Why or why not?

    Answers may vary. It is not satisfying because it ends rather abruptly, wrapping up Colin's story, but leaving readers wondering how the arrival of Archibald would affect Mary.

20. Can you see evidence of *The Secret Garden* influencing other stories and literature?

    Some claim that *The Secret Garden* provided inspiration for the rose garden imagery in *The Four Quartets*, by T.S. Eliot. It is also said that *The Secret Garden* was a childhood favorite of C.S. Lewis, who might have been inspired with Burnett's use of the

Robin, when he wrote in *The Lion the Witch and the Wardrobe*, "Still— a robin, you know. They're good birds in all the stories I've ever read. I'm sure a robin wouldn't be on the wrong side." Also, contemporary children's fiction writer, Katherine Paterson is said to have been inspired by *The Secret Garden* when she wrote her book *Bridge to Terabithia.*

21. Does Burnett's depictions of nature and Springtime match up with the way the world is?

Burnett's portrayal of nature teeters toward the sentimental side. Once she brings the sun out and Winter becomes Spring, there is a distinct lack of evil or brutality within the garden. This simply doesn't line up with the way the world is. Granted, she was trying to capture goodness and real sweetness, but those aspects, as true and real as they are, exist within a fallen framework. A rose still has thorns, robin's eggs are poached by other animals, and all that pollen in the air brings on allergies. Ask any mother and she'll tell you giving birth is painful. Re-birth is no exception. Not for humanity or creation.

FURTHER DISCUSSION AND REVIEW

Master what you have read by reviewing and integrating the different elements of this classic.

SETTING AND CHARACTERS

Be able to compare and contrast the personalities (including strengths, weaknesses, and mannerisms) of each character. Which characters change over the course of the novel? Which do not?

PLOT

Be able to describe the beginning, middle, and end of the book along with specific details that move the plot forward and make it compelling. This includes the success or downfall (or both) of each character.

CONFLICT

Go through the character list and describe the tension between any and all main characters. Then, think about whether any characters have internal conflict (in their own minds). Is there any overt conflict (fighting), or conflict with impersonal forces?

THEME STATEMENTS

Be able to describe what this classic is telling us about the world. Is the message true? What truth can we take from the plot, characters, conflict, and themes (even if the author didn't believe that truth)? Do any objects take on added meaning because of repetition or their place in the story (i.e., do any objects become symbols)? How does the author use perspective, tone, and irony to tell the truth?

- A Mother's influence is inescapable and will always affect her children whether she is good or bad, present or absent.
- A little slap upside the head, friends, fresh air and exercise are sometimes the best medicine for a bad attitude.
- Cheerfulness is not the same as wishful thinking. There are health benefits for the former, stupidity and embarrassment for the latter.
- Finally, compose your own theme statement about some element, large or small, of this classic. Then, use the Bible and common sense to assess the truth of that theme statement.

A NOTE FROM THE PUBLISHER:
TAKING THE CLASSICS QUIZ

Once you have finished the worldview guide, you can prepare for the end-of-book test. Each test will consist of a short-answer section on the book itself and the author, a short-answer section on plot and the narrative, and a long-answer essay section on worldview, conflict, and themes.

Each quiz, along with other helps, can be downloaded for free at www.canonpress.com/ClassicsQuizzes. If you have any questions about the quiz or its answers or the Worldview Guides in general, you can contact Canon Press at service@canonpress.com or 208.892.8074.

ABOUT THE AUTHOR

Amanda Ryan is a stay-at-home mom who teaches literature for Logos Online School and has written for Economic Modeling Specialists International. She has B.A.s in English and Music from the University of California and an M.A. in Theology and Letters from New Saint Andrews College. She and her husband Danny have two children.

www.ingramcontent.com/pod-product-compliance
Ingram Content Group UK Ltd.
Pitfield, Milton Keynes, MK11 3LW, UK
UKHW020416250726
13967UKWH00007B/2665

9 781947 644212